THE cRaZiest CHRISTMAS

EVeR!

SCHOLASTIC
SYDNEY AUCKLAND NEW YORK TORONTO LONDON MEXICO CITY
NEW DELHI HONG KONG BUENOS AIRES PUERTO RICO

Scholastic Australia
An imprint of Scholastic Australia Pty Limited
PO Box 579 Gosford NSW 2250
ABN 11 000 614 577
www.scholastic.com.au

Part of the Scholastic Group
Sydney • Auckland • New York • Toronto • London • Mexico City • New Delhi • Hong Kong • Buenos Aires • Puerto Rico

Published by Scholastic Australia in 2020.

Jokes by Jim Dewar.
Illustrations by Chad Mitchell.

A catalogue record for this book is available from the National Library of Australia

ISBN 978-1-74383-491-6

Typeset in Hank BT.

Printed by McPherson's Printing Group, Maryborough, VIC.

Scholastic Australia's policy, in association with McPherson's Printing Group, is to use papers that are renewable and made efficiently with wood from responsibly managed sources, so as to minimise its environmental footprint.

The paper in this book is FSC® certified. FSC® promotes environmentally responsible, socially beneficial and economically viable management of the world's forests.

21 22 23 24 25 / 2

FOREWORD

I'm Dean, one of the Camp Quality Puppets. You've probably heard of me! I'm basically famous. OK, maybe not quite yet . . . but I'm working on it! After all, I'm writing this letter at the start of this super cool joke book for you, so I'm kind of a big deal.

You may have seen me at your school telling awesome jokes and teaching kids about cancer. When I grow up, I want to be a world-famous stand-up comedian, so I loooove joke books, just like this one. I think jokes are really awesome and making people laugh is my superpower.

You see, my mum has cancer. And some days she feels really sad. She feels sick and she doesn't have much energy. She can't go to the park with me and do all the fun stuff we used to do. So when she has a bad day, I just want to make her smile. That's why I started telling jokes. My jokes make her laugh so much, and when she's laughing, she forgets all about cancer and all the things she can't do right now. It makes her happy again.

This joke book you hold in your hand now is not just a book. It's something that makes people smile and laugh and feel good. But before you read all the other jokes in this book, let me try out some of mine on you, so you can see why I'm almost, nearly famous. Drum roll, please!

Q: How do you talk to a giant?

A: By using big words!

Q: What do you call a dog magician?

A: A Labracadabrador.

Have you stopped laughing yet? Maybe you could become my new number one fan (after my mum). You could even book me for a live show at your school, with my friends Kylie and Mel, the other Camp Quality puppets! It's easy—just tell your teacher or an adult at home to get in touch with Camp Quality at campquality.org.au or on 02 9876 0500. Not only will we make you laugh, we'll teach you about cancer and you can even get a selfie with me before I hit the big time! #campquality #laughteristhebestmedicine

Bye, everyone! Happy joke times!

Dean

Q: When Dasher joked about Santa getting a second sleigh, what did Santa reply?

A: 'Pull the other one.'

Q: When Sir Lancelot lost his voice at Christmas, what did his friends sing?

A: *Silent Knight.*

Charlotte: 'Mummy, why is Blitzen carrying an umbrella?'

Mummy: 'He thinks it's going to rain, dear.'

Q: Who gives young sharks their Christmas presents?

A: Santa Jaws.

Q: What do witches sing at Christmas?

A: 'Jingle spells, jingle spells.'

Q: Will Santa reveal his secret route through the freezing northern lands?

A: Snow way!!

Q: Why is a foot a thoughtful Christmas present?

A: Because it's a good stocking filler.

Q: What do pelicans sing at Christmas?

A: 'Jingle bills, jingle bills.'

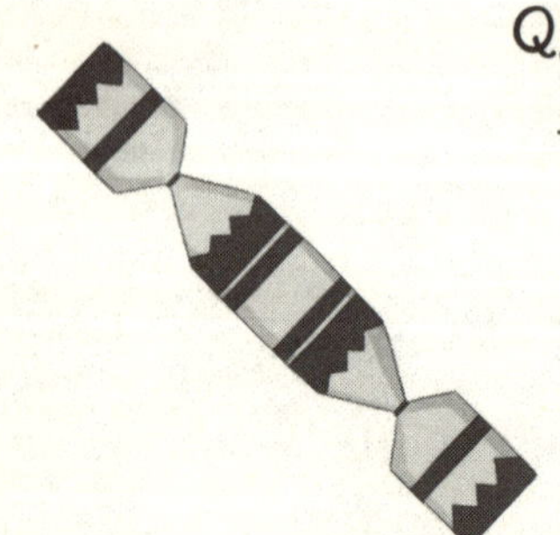

Q: What is Santa wearing when he comes down a chimney?

A: His best soot.

Q: What Christmas carol do dogs sing?

A: Bark, the *Herald Angels Sing.*

Q: What did Santa say when he spotted three gardening tools?

A: 'Hoe, hoe, hoe!'

Q: What do snowmen love to do on the weekend?

A: Chill out.

Q: Who do you get when you cross Santa with a private eye?

A: Santa Clues.

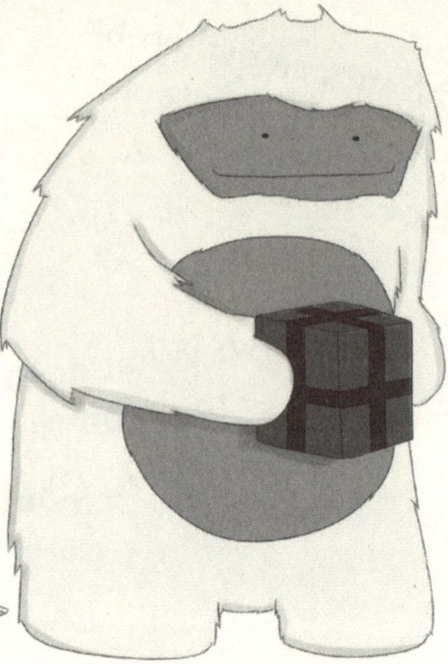

Santa: 'Has the Abominable Snowman visited?'
Mrs Claus: 'Not Yeti.'

Q: What Christmas carol do guitarists sing?
A: *Strum, All Ye Faithful.*

Q: Who gives young crabs their Christmas presents?
A: Santa Claws.

Q: What Christmas carol do good batsmen sing?

A: *Runs in Royal David's City.*

Q: Where do reindeer go when they lose their tails?

A: A re-tail shop.

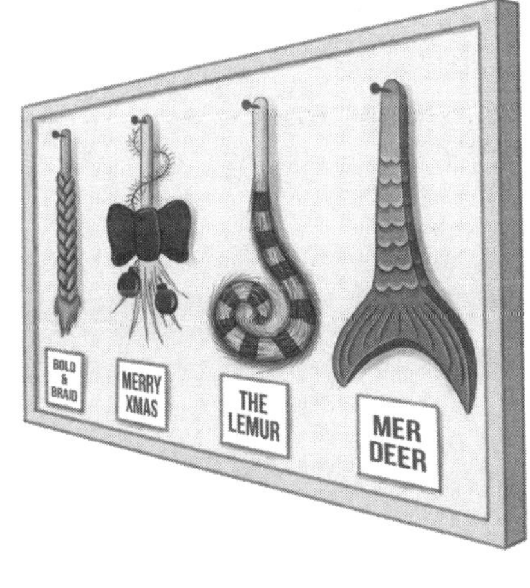

Q: Why are cold knitters like Christmas trees?

A: They keep dropping needles.

Q: What Christmas carol do scared batsmen sing?

A: *Duck the Balls.*

Q: Who gives pups their Christmas presents?

A: Santa Paws.

Q: Why do mummies enjoy Christmas so much?

A: They love all the wrapping.

Q: What do snowmen wear on their heads?

A: Ice caps.

Q: What Christmas carol do horses sing?

A: A Neigh in a Manger.

Q: What's the best Christmas present you can get?

A: A ruined drum—you just can't beat it!

Q: What Christmas carol do bees sing?

A: *We Three Stings.*

Q: What do you get when you cross Frosty the Snowman with an archer?

A: Frosty the Bowman.

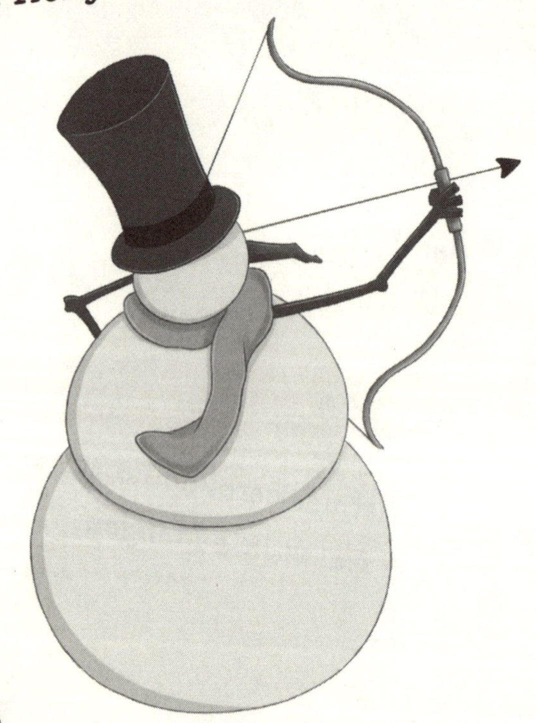

Q: What do you get if you cross a duck with mistletoe?

A: A Christmas quacker.

Q: What do you call Santa when he melts?
A: Santa Thaws.

Q: Who does Santa have to beware of while delivering presents on Australia's east coast?
A: The Great Barrier Thief.

Q: What Christmas carol do umbrellas sing?
A: The Brolly and the Ivy.

Dasher: 'What's that reindeer doing to Santa's sleigh?'
Dancer: 'She's just Vixen the harness.'

Q: What Christmas carol do caring shepherds sing?
A: *While Shepherds Washed Their Flocks by Night.*

Q: What do you call Santa when he takes a break?
A: Santa Pause.

Q: If Santa's little helpers take pics of themselves, what are they called?
A: Elfies.

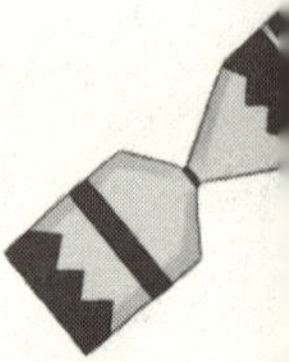

Q: What does a snowman have for breakfast?

A: **Snowflakes.**

Q: How do Santa's reindeer know what day it is?

A: **They check their calen-deer.**

Q: What Christmas carol do ocean monsters with chainsaws sing?

A: ***I Saw Three Ships.***

Q: What do you call a snowman when he gets really old?

A: **A puddle.**

Q: Why is Santa so jolly?

A: He only works one day a year.

Q: Who do you get when you cross Santa with a clothing store owner?

A: Santa Clothes.

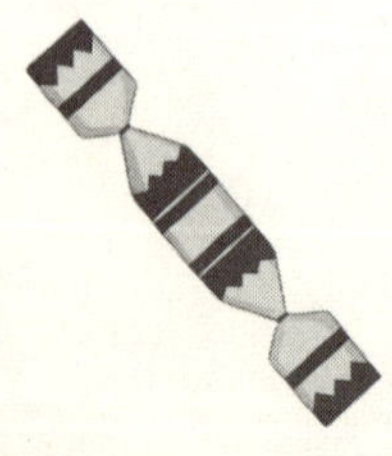

Q: How much does it cost to have a chimney installed for Santa's visit?

A: Nothing, it's on the house.

Q: What do schools of fish sing at Christmas time?

A: Christmas corals.

Charlie: 'Mummy, why is Dasher wearing a crown?'

Mummy: 'He thinks he's going to reign, dear.'

Q: How does Mrs Frog tell her little one to unwrap its Christmas present?

A: Rippit! Rippit! Rippit!

Q: Why are there only twenty-five letters in Santa's alphabet?

A: There is Noel.

Q: What do crabs and Christmas have in common?

A: Sandy claws.

Q: What do cattle hang on their Christmas trees?

A: Horn-aments.

Knock, knock!

Who's there?

Snow.

Snow who?

Snow business of yours!

Q: Why did Santa get booked on Christmas Eve?

A: His sleigh was parked in a snow parking zone.

Q: What's Santa's favourite carol?

A: *O Holly Night.*

Q: What do Australian wild dogs sing at Christmas time?
A: 'Dingo bells, dingo bells.'

Q: What type of music do Santa's elves love?
A: Wrap music.

Knock, knock!
Who's there?
Wayne.
Wayne who?
Wayne in a manger.

Q: What appears right at the end of Christmas?

A: S.

Q: How can you tell when Santa is close by?

A: You can sense his presents.

Q: Did you hear about the ghosts' Christmas party?

A: It was a scream.

Q: What did Santa and Mrs Claus hang over their baby's cot?

A: A snowmobile.

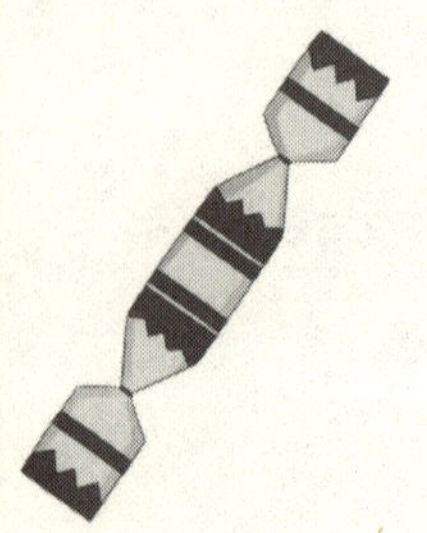

Q: What might you catch if you eat sparkly Christmas tree decorations?

A: Tinsel-itis.

Q: What athletic event does Santa excel at?

A: Pole vault.

Q: What do cranky mice give each other at Christmas?

A: Cross-mouse presents.

Q: What do sheep sing at Christmas time?

A: *We Wish Ewe a Merry Christmas.*

Q: Why does Santa choose to go down chimneys?

A: It really soots him.

Knock, knock!

Who's there?

Cam.

Cam who?

Cam all ye faithful.

Q: What does Santa sing to his helpers at Christmas time?

A: Have Your Elf a Merry Little Christmas.

Elf: 'Is Santa busy?'

Mrs Claus: 'Yes, he's completely snowed under.'

Q: Why does Santa use reindeer to pull his sleigh in Australia?

A: Because kangaroos can't fly.

Q: Why is Santa's sleigh able to travel so far?

A: It has long-distance runners.

Q: Why would Santa make a good actor?

A: He has a lot of presents and his delivery is excellent.

Elf: 'Can I see Santa please?'
Mrs Claus: 'Not at the present time.'

Q: What's Santa's nationality?
A: He lives at the North Pole so he must be North Polish.

Q: Did you hear about the owls' Christmas party?
A: It was a hoot.

Knock, knock!

Who's there?

Don.

Don who?

Don open until Christmas.

Mrs Claus: 'Why are you upset with some of the elves?'

Santa: 'They didn't do their gnome-work.'

Q: Where does Santa recruit his little helpers?

A: From the Antarctic ice elves.

Q: How do snowmen get around?

A: They ride their icicles.

Elf: 'Why hasn't Santa's sleigh moved yet?'

Mrs Claus: 'Because of the terribly heavy rain, dear.'

Q: What happens if an elf misbehaves?

A: Santa gives him the sack.

Q: What did one icicle say to the other icicle?

A: Ice to meet you.

Q: What do vampires sing at the end of their Christmas party?

A: *Auld Fang Syne.*

Q: What's green, covered in tinsel and croaks?

A: A mistle-toad.

THE REINDEER RACE

Christmas is over and Santa's work's done,
It's time for his reindeer to chill and have fun.
Santa says, 'Let's have a real reindeer race!
There's no sleigh to pull—and a prize for first place!'

They're off! And it's Dasher who dashes ahead,
But he runs out of puff as his face turns bright red.

Old Vixen takes off on a shortcut she knows,
But trips on a tree root and over she goes!

Dancer soon waltzes right
through to the lead . . .

Then Comet zooms past
her at shooting-star speed!

But Comet burns up and falls out of the race,
And Cupid and Donner compete for first place.
Cupid drops back, Donner leads by a foot,
But now Blitzen's storming along in pursuit!
'I'll blitz 'em,' thinks Blitzen, but on the last corner
He slips and he slides . . . and he slams into Donner!
Look there! Here comes Prancer! See how he glows!
He streaks to the finish—and wins by a nose!

Q: What did Dancer say when he realised he was late?

A: 'Oh, deer me.'

Knock, knock!

Who's there?

Arthur.

Arthur who?

Arthur any mince pies left?

Q: What do you call cutting down pine trees in December?

A: Christmas chopping.

Elf: 'Is Santa happy with my work?'

Mrs Claus: 'Yes, he's wrapped.'

Dancer: 'What's wrong with Vixen?'
Prancer: 'She's terribly upset. She's just discovered she's really a fox.'

Q: What payment system do Santa's little helpers use?
A: ELFTPOS.

Q: What do you call a badly-behaved elf that no longer works for Santa?

A: A rebel without a Claus.

Q: How come Frosty the snowman disappeared so fast?

A: He tried out Santa's sauna.

Q: Why did Santa ban his little helpers from riding on his sleigh?
A: He had elf and safety concerns.

Elf: 'Why didn't Santa deliver presents to the String family?'
Mrs Claus: 'Because they've been very knotty.'

Q: Does Santa love his reindeer?
A: Yes, they're deer to his heart.

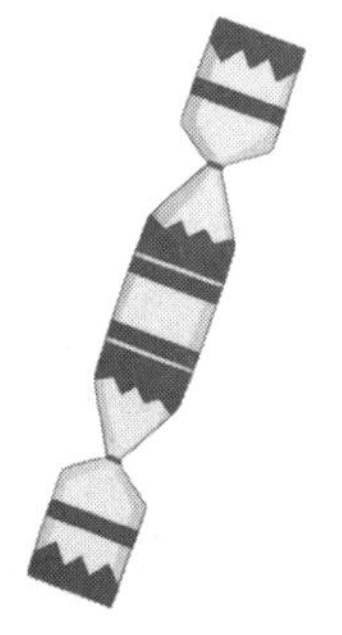

Knock, knock!
Who's there?
Murray.
Murray who?
Murray Christmas to you!

Elf: 'Why didn't Santa deliver presents to the Bell family?'

Mrs Claus: 'Because they get into trouble chime and chime again.'

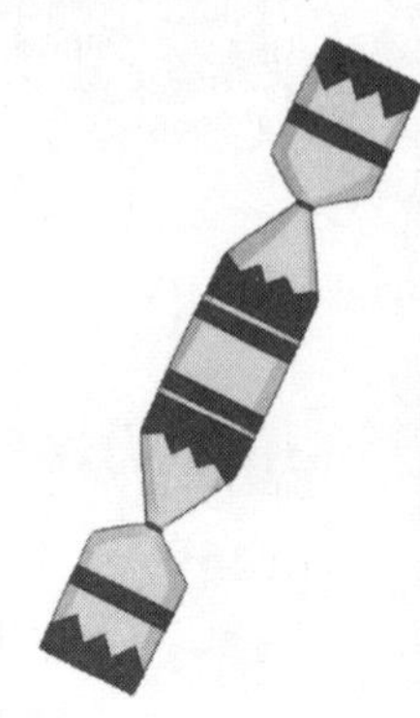

Q: What do you call the fear of getting stuck in a chimney?

A: Claustrophobia.

Q: How do Santa's reindeer amuse themselves in their spare time?

A: **They play stable-tennis.**

Q: What Christmas creatures have one hundred legs?

A: **Santapedes.**

Q: What do ghosts sing at Christmas time?

A: ***I'm Dreaming of a Fright Christmas.***

Q: What's Santa's favourite Christmas song?

A: *Ho-Ho-Ho-ly Night.*

Q: Why does Santa's nose go red and sore?

A: In the icy breezes he wheezes and sneezes and it freezes.

Q: What does Santa do when his reindeers' antlers get too big and heavy?

A: He calls in the antler dismantler.

Santa: 'What would you like for Christmas?'

Kid: 'Lots of things. For full details, check out my website.'

Q: What do Australian frogs wear to Christmas parties on the beach?

A: Open-toad sandals.

Knock, knock!

Who's there?

Anna.

Anna who?

Anna partridge in a pear tree.

Elf: 'Why didn't Santa deliver presents to the Lamb family?'

Mrs Claus: 'Because they've been so baaaaa-d.'

Knock, knock!

Who's there?

Wal King.

Wal King who?

Wal King in a winter wonderland.

Q: What do sheep send to shepherds at Christmas time?

A: Season's bleatings.

Q: What's a guitarist's favourite Christmas song?

A: *Santa Claus Is Strumming to Town.*

Father: 'That train set looks terrific. I'll buy it.'

Salesperson: 'Wonderful. I'm sure your son will love it!'

Father: 'Hmm, you could be right. In that case, I'll take two.'

Mrs Claus: 'How are you feeling?'

Elf: 'I wasn't well for a few days, but now I'm in the best of elf.'

Q: What's red and white and bounces up and down?

A: Santa on a jumping castle.

Q: How do you decorate a rowing boat for Christmas?

A: Use lots of oar-naments.

Q: What happens when a snowman loses his temper?

A: He has a meltdown.

Q: What do Santa's little helpers get for doing an excellent job?

A: Santa-pplause.

Q: What's a horse's favourite Christmas song?

A: *The Twelve Neighs of Christmas.*

Q: Why was Santa upset when he arrived in Australia?

A: He heard about Christmas in July and thought it would double his workload.

Nick: 'Is it true that reindeer have amazing eyesight?'

Nicole: 'Well, have you ever seen one wearing glasses?'

Q: Which South American country did Santa find really cool on his rounds?

A: Chile.

Q: Mr Elf likes to play on his toboggan. What's his favourite song?

A: *The Itsy Bitsy Slider.*

Q: Why do Santa's elves wear pointy hats?

A: So that their pointy ears don't feel lonely.

Q: What do you call an igloo without a toilet?

A: An ig.

Q: Why is Santa unpopular when playing cricket?

A: He does a lot of sledging.

Q: What did Santa have fitted to his sleigh while in Central Australia?

A: Alice springs.

Q: What do snowmen call their little ones?

A: Chill-dren.

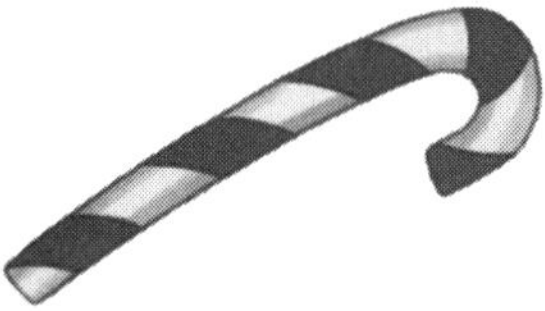

Q: What do you do if Santa gets stuck in your chimney?

A: Ring triple ho!

Q: What prickly mammal likes to ride in Santa's sleigh?

A: The sledge-hog.

Q: Where do Santa's elves go dancing?

A: A snow ball.

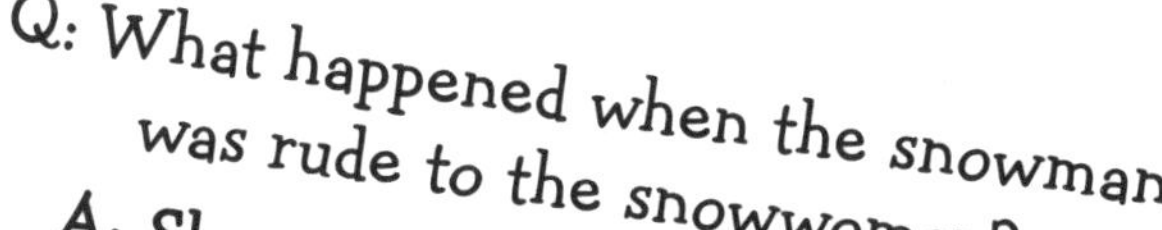

Q: What happened when the snowman was rude to the snowwoman?

A: She gave him an icy stare then the cold shoulder.

Q: What do you get if you cross an octopus with a Christmas turkey?

A: Enough drumsticks for everyone.

Q: What's the best thing to give your parents at Christmas?

A: A list of everything you want.

Q: Does an elf plan for the future?

A: No, he lives only for the present.

Q: Where does Santa Claus keep his clothes?

A: In his claus-et.

Tilly: 'What is the reason for reindeer?'

Billy: 'It makes the grass grow, darling.'

Q: What huge animal lives in the forest where Christmas trees grow?

A: The pine-oceros.

Q: What is red and white and goes up and down, up and down, up and down?

A: Santa on a seesaw.

Q: How do Santa's elves get around?

A: In a minibus.

Q: What is Santa when he stops moving?

A: Still Santa.

Q: What do Santa's elves watch on TV?

A: Miniseries.

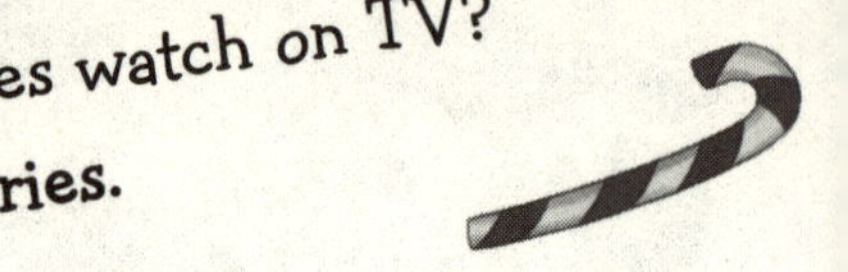

Q: What prize did the handsome husky win at the dog show?

A: 'Best in Snow.'

Q: What did the tinsel say to the dangly decorations on the Christmas tree?

A: 'Aren't you tired of just hanging around?'

Q: How do you scare a snowman?

A: Approach him with a hair dryer.

Q: Why does Santa prefer hearts and diamonds?

A: He likes red suits.

Q: Mr Elf keeps the sleighbells in good condition. What's his favourite song?

A: *Tinkle, Tinkle, Little Star.*

Q: How did the snow globe feel after being played with?

A: A little shaken.

Knock, knock!

Who's there?

Mary and Abby.

Mary and Abby who?

Mary Christmas and Abby New Year!

Q: How do you dress up a ship for Christmas?

A: Use lots of deck-orations.

Q: What's a secret agent's favourite Christmas food?

A: Mince spies.

Q: How did the cow decide on its Christmas present?

A: It chose something from a Christmas cattle-ogue.

Q: How does Mrs Claus organise her pantry?

A: With Santa's shelves.

Q: When Santa was a kid at school what did he like best?

A: Snow-and-tell.

Q: Why did the Christmas ornament love woods and forests?

A: It was hooked on trees its whole life.

Q: Why don't crabs exchange presents at Christmas?

A: They're really shellfish.

Q: If Santa has eleven elves working for him and he hires an extra one, what's that one called?

A: The twelf.

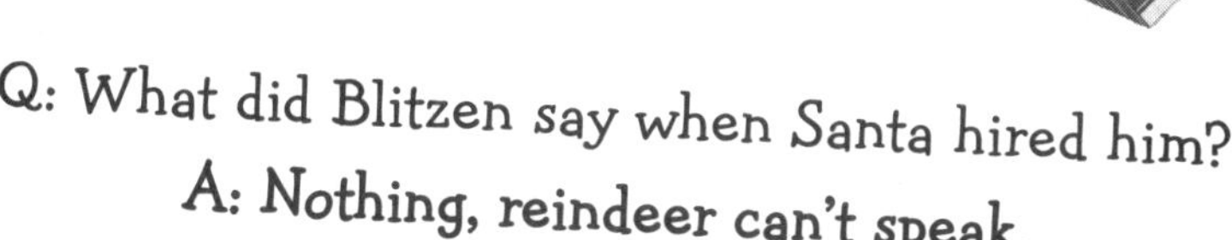

Q: What did Blitzen say when Santa hired him?

A: Nothing, reindeer can't speak.

Q: Why do goats get upset with Santa at Christmas?

A: He promises that every kid will get a present, but baby goats keep missing out.

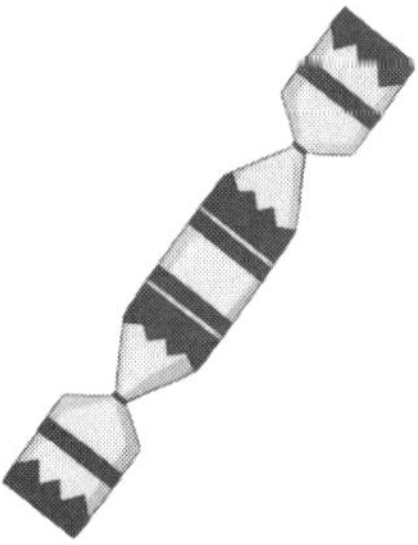

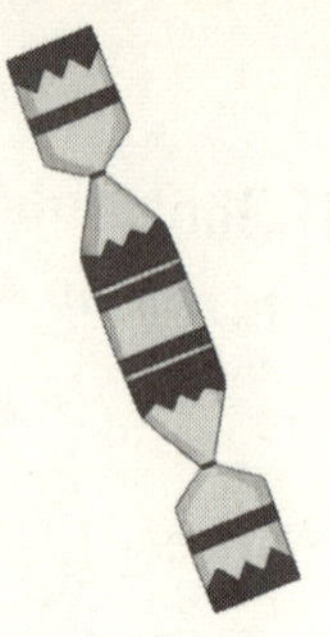

Santa: 'Well then, Jessica, what would you like for Christmas?'

Jessica: 'Didn't you get my email?!'

Q: Why didn't the snowflake do what the teacher asked?

A: It just wouldn't glisten.

Q: What's red and grey and pulls Santa's sleigh in Australia?

A: A red-nosed koala.

Knock, knock!

Who's there?

Rabbit.

Rabbit who?

Rabbit neatly—it's a Christmas present.

Q: What do you call a gang of snowflakes?

A: A snowball.

Q: What did one blizzard say to the other blizzard?

A: Do you get my drift?

Bella: 'We had Grandad for Christmas dinner.'

Stella: 'Really? We had ham.'

Q: What do horses do at Christmas?

A: They share presents with their neigh-bours.

Q: What do sheep sing at Christmas parties when Santa arrives?

A: *Fleece a Jolly Good Fellow.*

Q: What should you say to the salt and pepper at Christmas dinner?

A: 'Seasoning's greetings!'

Q: What colour is a young reindeer?

A: Fawn.

Q: Why did the boat crew get into trouble at Christmas time?

A: They put a ferry on top of their Christmas tree.

NAUGHTY ELVES

The elves get up to mischief
At the back of Santa's sleigh.
They tie it to the nearest tree,
It just can't move away!
The reindeer pull their hearts out,
As Santa bellows, 'GO!'
But Santa's sleigh won't budge an inch,
It's stuck there in the snow.
But then the elves feel sorry,
So they cut the rope right through.
The sleigh flies forward suddenly,
And Santa flies out too!

He ends up in a pine tree,
All red and scratched and bruised.
The toys are scattered everywhere,
His reindeer are confused.
The elves soon learn their lesson:
To get things back on track,
They need to work like crazy
And refill Santa's sack.
So, kids, if Santa's late this year,
Please don't upset yourselves.
If you've been good, the ones to blame
Are Santa's naughty elves!

Q: What do bits of wood sing at Christmas time?

A: *Splinter Wonderland.*

Q: What do you call Santa as he prepares to shave?

A: Lather Christmas.

Q: What do you call a kangaroo wearing a Santa hat?

A: A Christmas jumper.

Q: What do you call a reindeer in the outback?

A: Lost.

Q: What kind of TV did the ghost want for Christmas?

A: A wide-scream TV.

Q: What do you call Frosty the Snowman when he's in his little boat?

A: Frosty the Rowman.

Q: Why don't reindeer make good dancers?

A: Because they have two left feet.

Q: Why did Ozzie get into trouble with his little sister on Christmas Day?

A: He threw a few prawns on the barbie doll.

Q: Which Christmas carol is all about a sticky ruler?

A: *Glued King Wenceslas.*

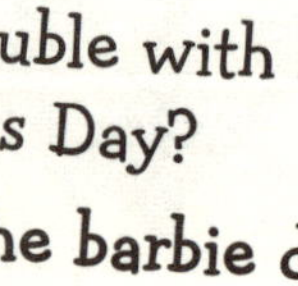

Q: Why is Santa such a good cricketer?
A: He can make the trickiest of deliveries look easy.

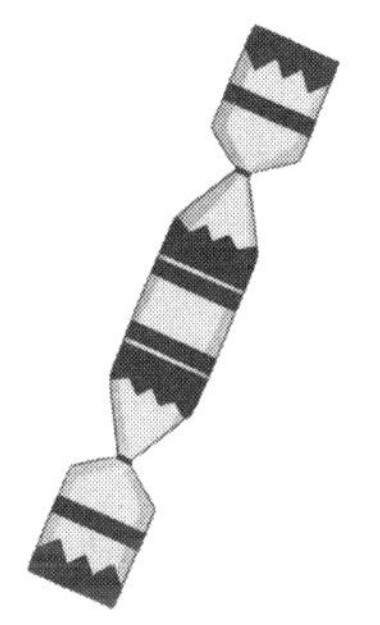

Q: What goes 'OH, OH, OH?'
A: Santa doing the moonwalk.

Q: What happens to Santa's sleighbells in the Australian outback?
A: The ding-goes.

Q: How do you know carol-singers are approaching?
A: They jingle all the way.

Q: Why do Santa's elves like to party in a blizzard?

A: Because they know it'll be a real blast.

Q: How do chickens send Christmas cards?

A: In hen-velopes.

Q: What do you call a legendary snow creature with well-developed tummy muscles?

A: The Abdominal Snowman.

Q: How do we know Santa is an expert at karate?

A: He's got a black belt.

Q: Why did Danny wear only one gumboot to the Christmas party?

A: He heard there was only a fifty per cent chance of snow.

Q: What do you call a young deer that runs around and rings?

A: A mobile fawn.

Q: What is red and white and noisy?

A: Santa with a drum kit.

Q: What did Santa call out to all the toys on Christmas Eve?

A: 'It's getting late, everyone—sack time!'

Q: Which teacher hangs from the ceiling at Christmas?

A: Miss L Toe.

Knock, knock!

Who's there?

Wenceslas.

Wenceslas who?

Wenceslas bus due on Christmas Eve?

Q: Mr Elf can never make up his mind. What's his favourite song?

A: *Rock-a-Bye Maybe*.

Q: Why did no-one bid for Prancer and Dancer at the auction?

A: They were two deer.

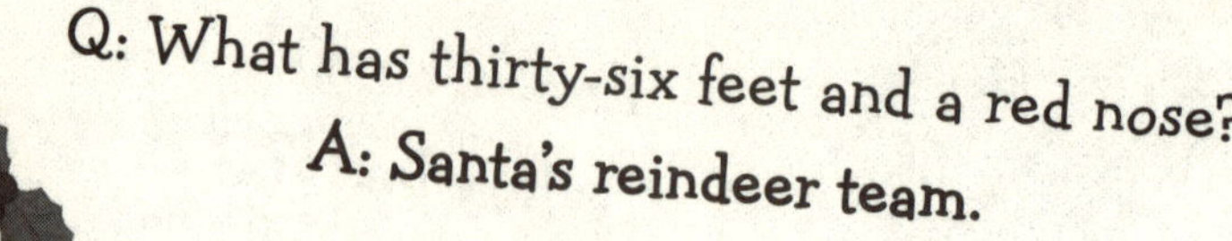

Q: What has thirty-six feet and a red nose?

A: Santa's reindeer team.

Q: How does Santa keep track of all the chimneys he's been down?

A: He keeps a log book.

First Christmas tree: 'You need to spruce yourself up a bit!'

Second Christmas tree: 'I'm pine the way I am!'

Third Christmas tree: 'What are you two arguing fir?'

Q: Why didn't the butterfly go to the Christmas party?

A: It was a moth ball.

Q: What do polar bears have for Christmas lunch?

A: Icebergers with chilli sauce.

Q: Why didn't the skeleton go to the Christmas party?

A: It had no body to go with.

Elf 1: 'Can I borrow ten dollars from you?'

Elf 2: 'Sorry, but I'm a little short.'

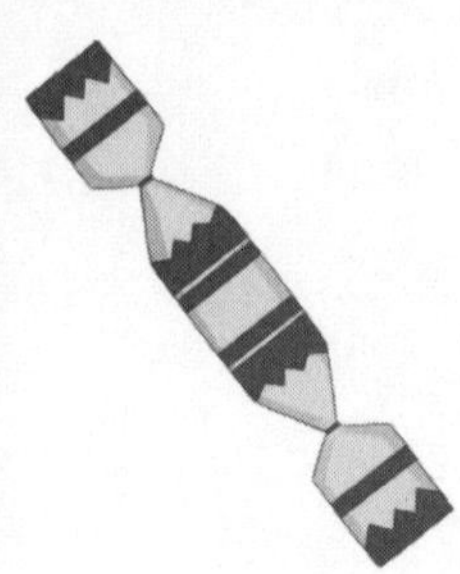

Q: In which Australian city can you hear Santa laughing?
A: Ho-Ho-Hobart.

Q: What did Santa say when his sleigh almost collided with a tree?
A: 'Wow! That was a Claus shave!'

Q: What goes red, white, SPLASH?
A: Surfing Santa falling off his board.

Q: What's black and white and red?

A: A zebra in a Santa suit.

Q: How do we know Santa is such a good race car driver?

A: He always starts from pole position.

Mum: 'Liam, why are you crossing "train set" off your Christmas wish list?'

Liam: 'I don't need one anymore—I found a brand-new one in the cupboard!'

Q: What do you call a reindeer who tilts?

A: Eileen.

Q: How many presents can Santa's elves pack into his empty sack?

A: Only one! After that, his sack won't be empty.

Santa: 'I taught Comet to play chess.'

Mrs Claus: 'He must be very smart!'

Santa: 'Not really. I won two games out of three.'

Q: What did one Christmas candle say to the other Christmas candle?

A: 'Do you fancy going out tonight?'

Q: What do you call an elf running to escape a snowstorm?

A: A yelping helper belting helter-skelter for shelter.

Q: What falls from a great height at the North Pole but never gets hurt?

A: Snow.

Q: Mr Elf enjoys carving little figures. What are his favourite songs?

A: *Whittle Miss Muffet* and *Whittle Jack Horner*.

Q: Why was the duck welcome at Christmas parties?

A: It was always quacking jokes.

Katie: 'Are Santa and Mrs Claus coming to English class this afternoon?'

Teacher: 'No, Jeanie. Why do you ask?'

Katie: 'Yesterday you said you'd introduce us to clauses today.'

Knock, knock!

Who's there?

Arthur.

Arthur who?

Arthur any presents for me?

Q: What do sausage dogs sing at Christmas time?

A: *Dachshund Through the Snow.*

Q: Why were there no brussels sprouts on the Christmas lunch menu?

A: The chef decided to give peas a chance.

Q: How did the Christmas crackers' party go?

A: It went off with a BANG!

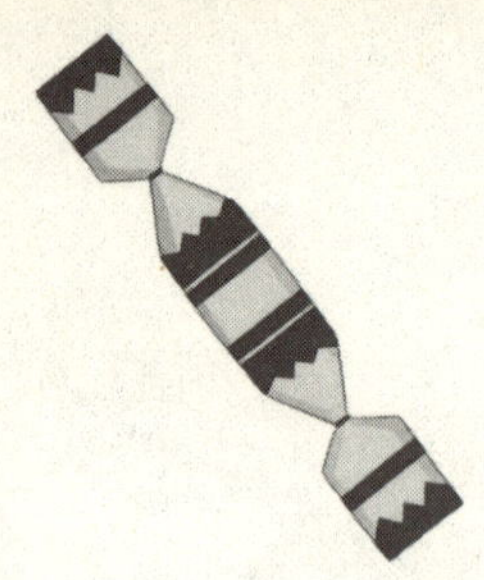

Q: What's red and white and zooms across the night sky?

A: Santa Claus.

Q: Where do elves go if they are sick?

A: The local elf centre.

Q: How was Santa given the chance to score a goal in the football match?

A: The Ghost of Christmas passed.

Q: What did the naughty puppy say to the Christmas tree?

A: It's been nice gnawing you.

Q: What do you call Frosty the Snowman at Christmas in Australia?

A: A miracle.

Q: What do you call Father Christmas at the beach?

A: Sandy Claus.

Q: What carol did the Christmas diners sing when their food was late?

A: *O Come All Ye Plateful.*

Q: Why did the referee stop the royal boxing match?

A: Good King Wenceslas looked out.

Q: What do you get when you cross a bee with a sleighbell?

A: A humdinger.

Q: What's green, covered in tinsel and can be made into bread?

A: Mistle-dough.

Q: Why is there a shortage of water at the North Pole?

A: No well, no well . . .

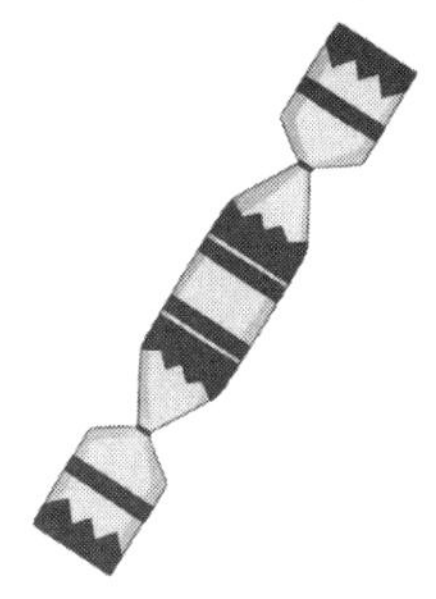

Q: How many chimneys has Santa climbed down?

A: Stacks!

Q: What do you call Frosty the Snowman when he's cutting the grass?

A: Frosty the Mowman.

Q: What's long and flat and sounds like an elf?

A: A shelf.

Knock, knock!

Who's there?

Harriet.

Harriet who?

Harriet all the Christmas cake!

Q: What did the tree bauble say to the Santa hat?

A: **'I'll hang around while you go on ahead.'**

Liam: 'I'd like lots of packets of bird seed for Christmas.'

Santa: 'How many birds do you have?'

Liam: 'None. I plan to grow some.'

Q: What happened to the dozen reindeer that Santa lost?

A: **Nobody's herd.**

Q: What's red and white, red and white, red and white . . .

A: **Santa caught in a revolving door.**

Q: Do you know how long reindeer should sleep?

A: Exactly the same way as short reindeer.

Customer: 'Do you have Christmas pudding on the menu today?'

Waiter: 'No, I cleaned it off.'

Q: Why did Mrs Claus shed a tear when Santa set off to deliver presents?

A: She just got a little Santa-mental.

Q: What is a crocodile's favourite Christmas party game?

A: Snap!

Q: What's red and white and has three wheels?

A: Santa riding a tricycle.

Q: What did the elves do when all the toys were ready for delivery?

A: They gave Santa the sack.

Q: How long do reindeers' legs have to be for them to be part of Santa's team?

A: Long enough to reach the ground.

Alex: 'Mum, can I have two canaries for Christmas?'

Mum: 'No, you'll have ham like the rest of us.'

Q: Who is Prancer's favourite singer?

A: Beyon-sleigh.

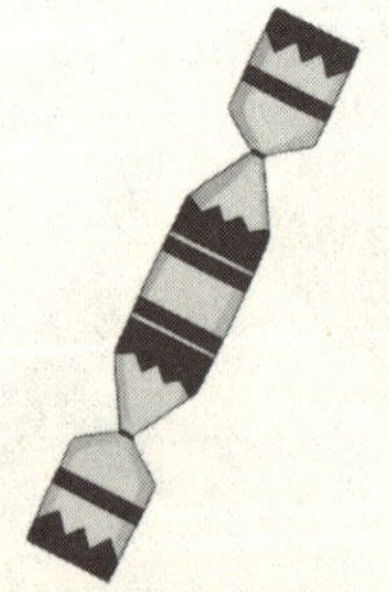

Q: Where does Santa practise climbing down chimneys?

A: A chim-nasium.

Q: Why is it impossible to keep a secret at the North Pole?

A: Because your teeth chatter.

Q: How can you make opening your Christmas presents last a lot longer?

A: Wear boxing gloves.

Q: How do you build a snowman in Australia at Christmas time?

A: With great difficulty!

Q: What goes 'Ho, Ho, Ho . . . OUCH!!!'?

A: Santa splitting his sides laughing!

Q: Is Santa planning to get a bigger workshop?

A: He's toying with the idea.

Q: Which reindeer likes to go to the disco?

A: Dancer.

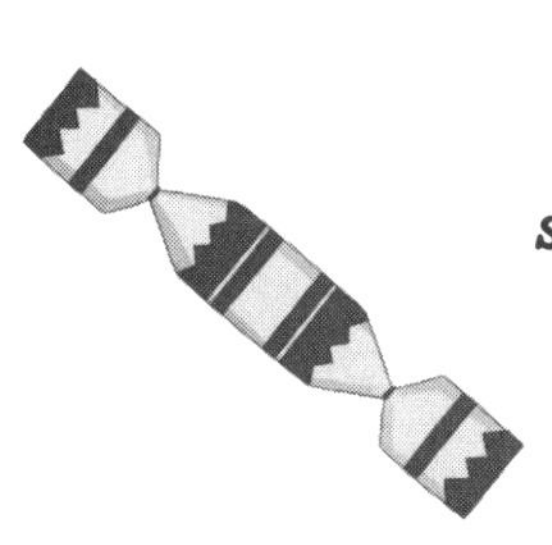

Q: What happens to Santa's sleigh when he gets sleepy?

A: Sleepy Santa's slick sleigh slowly slips and slides in the slush.

Q: What insect doesn't like Christmas?

A: A humbug.

Q: What do sharks sing at Christmas time?

A: *I'm Dreaming of a Great White Christmas.*

Q: Did Santa's new reindeer harness work out well over Christmas?

A: It passed the test with flying collars.

Q: What do angels say when they meet each other?

A: 'Halo there!'

Q: What do you get when you cross a Christmas tree with an ice cream?

A: A pine cone.

Q: Mr Elf loves sailing near the North Pole. What's his favourite song?

A: *Snow, Snow, Snow Your Boat.*

Q: What happened when Santa got rid of all his sleighbells?

A: He won the No-Bell Prize.

WHY SANTA'S TROUSERS WOULDN'T STAY UP
BY LUCY LASSTICK

SANTA DIDN'T STOP!
BY M T STOCKIN

EXTRA HELP FOR SANTA
BY ORSON CART

CHRISTMAS CAROLS
BY DEXTER HALLS

NO SCHOOL AT CHRISTMAS
BY HOLLY DAZE

Q: What do sea monsters have for Christmas dinner?

A: Fish and ships.

Santa: 'Why did you sell our vacuum cleaner?'

Mrs Claus: 'It was just collecting dust.'

KIDS' JOKES

Q: Where do snowmen keep their money?

A: In a snow bank.

Will, Age 8

Knock, knock.

Who's there?

Olive.

Olive who?

Olive the other reindeer.

Joe, Age 6

Q: What do you get when you cross a snowman and a dog?

A: Frostbite.

Tracey, Age 9

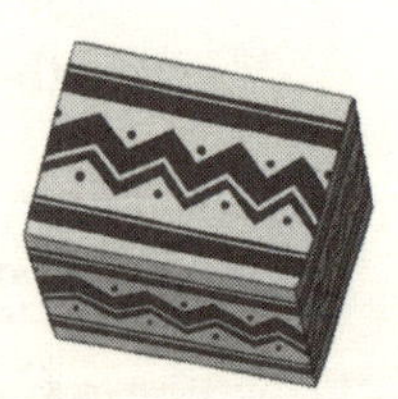

Q: What did one snowman say to the other snowman?

A: Do you smell carrots?

Sky, Age 5

MEET CAMP QUALITY

campquality.org.au

Camp Quality gives kids facing cancer the chance to be kids again.

Our services and programs are made specifically to help children 0–13 who are dealing with their own diagnosis, or the diagnosis of someone they love, like a brother, sister, mum or dad. We are there for them through the daily ups and downs of cancer, providing opportunities to laugh, make friends and have new adventures.

By creating positive memories, Camp Quality helps change the cancer story for kids and their families: in hospital, at home, at school and away from it all.

Our organisation does not currently receive any substantial financial support from the Australian Government nor any State or Territory Government, yet our services are provided completely free of charge, right across the country, to whoever needs them.

We believe laughter and optimism are essential to help our kids and their families not only cope but thrive.

At Camp Quality we love to share a joke. Can you tell?

HOW YOU CAN HELP!

It's easy to support Camp Quality and help kids facing cancer.

If you're looking for fun ways to get involved, why not get your school to hold a fundraising day for Camp Quality? **Fun Raise at School** is an awesome day where you can get together with your classmates, teachers and peers, whilst raising money for Camp Quality. Whether it's odd socks, crazy hair or a mufti day, you'd be helping our Aussie kids, and their families, who are facing the daily ups and down of cancer.

You can also support Camp Quality at home, work or your local club. Whether you do a bake sale, garage sale or sell homemade lemonade, raising money for our Camp Quality families can be as easy as it is fun! Creating memories that change the cancer story starts with you, so why not make a difference today!

If you need more information visit:
https://fundraise.campquality.org.au

JOKE SUBMISSION

Have you got a funny joke? Let us know and it might just end up being published in a joke book. How cool would that be?

Visit: **https://fundraise.campquality.org.au/jokesubmission** to submit your joke OR write it down and post it to us.

Camp Quality
My Joke
Locked Bag 7523
McMahons Point NSW 2060

Name .... Age ....

Address ....

....

State .... Postcode ....

Phone ....

Email ....

My cool joke ....

....

....

....

....

MAKE A DONATION

It's easy! Donate to Camp Quality in the following ways:

Online: campquality.org.au/donate
By phone: 1300 662 267
Or return this completed form:
By post: Camp Quality Limited, Locked Bag 7523, McMahons Point NSW 2060
By email: donorcare@campquality.org.au

Yes, I want to help kids facing cancer in Australia!

My details are:

Title: .... First name: .... Surname: ....

Address: ....

Suburb/Town: .... State: .... Postcode: ....

Phone/Mobile: .... Email: ....

My gift amount is: (please tick)

☐ $25 ☐ $50 ☐ Other: ....

Gift Frequency: ☐ One-off ☐ Monthly

I wish to make my payment by:

☐ Cheque / Money Order ☐ Mastercard ☐ Visa ☐ Amex

Card number: ☐☐☐☐ ☐☐☐☐ ☐☐☐☐ ☐☐☐☐

Expiry: ☐☐ / ☐☐ Name on card: ....

Your signature: .... Today's date: ....

All donations over $2 are tax deductible.
ABN 87 052 097 720